My First Stories

My Daddy's Footsteps

Text by François Barcelo

To Veda Rose, my little granddaughter, hoping your father will be better at being on time than I was.

Illustrations by Marc Mongeau

Every day at dawn, I hear the sound of his steps . . . To Arthur, the little thief who steals my sleep.

alphabet s o u p ™

an imprint of

WINDMILL BOOKS™

New York

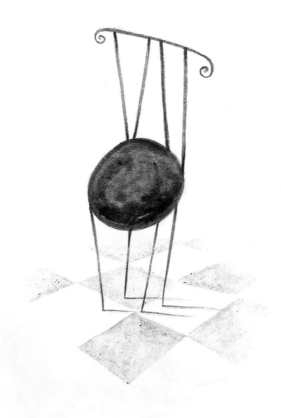

If there's one thing I don't like, it's eating dinner
without my father.
Mom tells me, "He works hard."
But I wonder, "What is he doing right now?"

Is he at the wrong house?
Did his tires go flat?

Is he glued to his chair?
Did he lose his wallet?

7

Did someone steal his pants?
Did he take the wrong flight?

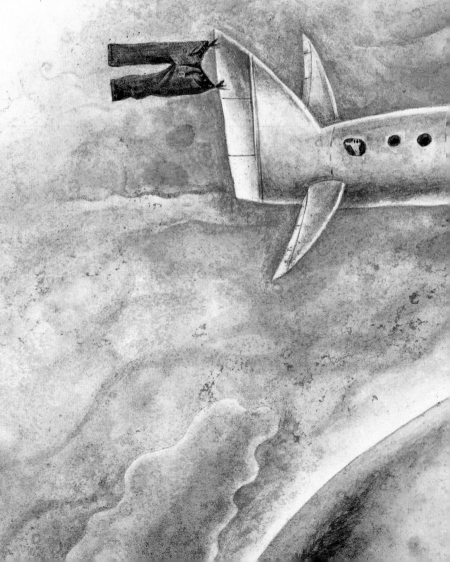

Is he stuck in a snowstorm?
Did a witch turn him into a frog?

Did the car break down?
Did he slip on a banana peel?

14

Is he hunting for treasure?
Did he run into a dinosaur?

16

Did someone steal his cell phone?
Is he riding a camel in the desert?

Does he have to fight burglars?
Or put out a fire?

Wait, I hear someone coming!
Finally, I can stop worrying . . .

21

. . . because I recognize those footsteps.
My daddy's footsteps.

23

Published in 2010 by Windmill Books, LLC
303 Park Avenue South, Suite # 1280, New York, NY 10010-3657

Adaptations to North American Edition © 2010 Windmill Books

Original title: Les pas de mon papa
Original Publisher: Les éditions Imagine inc
© François Barcelo / Marc Mongeau 2005
© Les éditions Imagine inc. 2005
English translation © Les éditions Imagine inc 2005

Publisher Cataloging in Publication

Barcelo, François, 1941-
        My daddy's footsteps. – North American ed. / text by François Barcelo ; illustrations by Marc Mongeau.
p. cm. – (My first stories)
Summary: A little boy imagines all the things that might make his daddy late coming home for dinner.
ISBN 978-1-60754-359-6 (lib.) – ISBN 978-1-60754-360-2 (pbk.)
ISBN 978-1-60754-361-9 (6-pack)
        1. Fathers—Juvenile fiction   2. Father and child—Juvenile fiction
3. Imagination—Juvenile fiction   [1. Fathers—Fiction   2. Father and child—Fiction   3. Imagination—Fiction   4. Worry—Fiction]   I. Mongeau, Marc   II. Title   III. Series
        [E]—dc22

Printed in the United States of America